don't get caught

By Eleanor Robins

SADDLEBACK
EDUCATIONAL PUBLISHING

CHOICES

SADDLEBACK
EDUCATIONAL PUBLISHING
www.sdlback.com

ISBN-13: 978-1-61651-592-8
ISBN-10: 1-61651-592-9
eBook: 978-1-61247-238-6

Printed in the U.S.A.

21 20 19 18 17   7 8 9 10 11

Meet the Characters from

don't get caught

Bree: sticks up for Max

Paris: dates Max and then Blake, is Bree's best friend

Blake: Trish's friend, wants to date Paris

Max: dates Paris, visits his grandparents

Trish: invites Paris to the homecoming game, sets Paris up with Blake, is Paris's cousin

chapter
1

It was Friday night. Paris was at a football game. She was with her boyfriend Max.

The game had just ended. Their team had won—just—by two points. Paris and Max started to walk to Max's car.

Max said, "That was a great game. But for a while I wasn't sure we would win."

Paris said, "I thought we might not win, either. I wish we could score more than two touchdowns in a game."

"Yeah. So do I," Max said.

The team had played five games. And they had scored only one or two touchdowns in each game.

"At least we have a good kicker," Paris said.

"You're right about that. He's one good kicker," Max said.

So far their kicker was having a good season. He'd kicked every extra point. And he'd kicked two field goals.

"We're lucky that the other team didn't have a good kicker, too. Or this game would have ended in a tie," Max said.

"I know," Paris said. A tie wasn't any fun. But it was better than losing.

Paris said, "Maybe we'll score more points in our next game."

"We can hope so. But I don't think our team is that good," Max said.

Paris didn't want to believe it. But

she thought Max was right. Their team wasn't that good. Paris and Max didn't talk for a few minutes.

Then Paris said, "I wish we had a game next weekend."

The team had a weekend off. Then they'd play their homecoming game the next week.

"I'm glad we don't have a game," Max said.

That surprised Paris. "Why?" she asked. Max liked football games as much as she did.

"I won't be here next weekend. I'm going to visit my grandparents," Max said.

"Again?" Paris asked.

She didn't mean to ask him that way. It just came out before she thought about it. And she didn't mean to ask it in that tone of voice.

Max stopped. He looked at Paris. "Does it upset you when I go to visit my grandparents?" Max asked.

"No," Paris said. That wasn't true. But Paris wouldn't tell Max that.

Paris said, "I was just surprised. You just went to see them two weekends ago."

"I care a lot about my grandparents. I told you that before. I like to visit them. They're a lot of fun to be with," Max said.

"I know you told me that before, Max. And I believe you care a lot about them," Paris said.

But was that the only reason he went to visit them so much? Paris didn't think it was. She thought there must be some other reason.

Was it because he was dating a girl who lived there? Did he think he could date a girl there? That she wouldn't find out?

Paris thought Max could be trusted. But she wasn't sure he could be. They started to walk again.

Max said, "You know I'll miss you next weekend. And I'll wish I was with you."

Then why was he going to see his grandparents? Paris wanted to ask him. But she didn't. She still thought it was because he was dating a girl there.

Was he? That was another question she wouldn't ask him.

chapter 2

It was the next Monday. Paris walked to the lunchroom. She always ate lunch with Bree. Bree was her best friend.

Paris had to study most of the weekend. She didn't have time to talk to Bree. So Paris really wanted to talk to her.

Bree was waiting for Paris in the hall outside of the lunchroom. Bree asked, "How were your tests, Paris?"

"Okay. I think I did all right on them," Paris said. Just her luck. She had two tests on the same day. Both were on Monday. And she had to study most of the weekend.

Paris and Bree quickly got their lunch. Then they hurried over to a table and sat down.

The girls ate for a few minutes. Then Paris asked, "Did you have fun this weekend?"

"Yes. Did you?" Bree asked.

"A little. But most of the time I had to study for those two tests. And that sure wasn't fun," Paris said.

Bree said, "Too bad. I'm glad you had the tests on Monday and not me. But at least you had time to go to the game Friday night. And that was too good a game to miss."

"You're right about that," Paris said. Paris had fun at the game. But she didn't have that good of a weekend. And it wasn't just because of the tests. It was also because Max was going to see his grandparents again.

Bree said, "We don't have a ballgame this weekend. So what will you and Max do this weekend? Or don't you know yet?"

"Nothing. That's what we'll do," Paris said.

Bree looked surprised. "Why, Paris? Did you have a fight? Why didn't you tell me?" she asked.

"We didn't have a fight. I would have told you right away if we had," Paris said.

"So why did you say you and Max would do nothing?" Bree asked.

"Max is going to see his grandparents again," Paris said. Paris knew she didn't sound happy about it. And she wasn't happy.

Bree said, "Max goes to see them a lot. He must care a lot about them."

"I guess so," Paris said.

Bree asked, "Why? Do you think he has another reason for going to see them?"

"I don't know," Paris said. Then Paris started to eat some more of her lunch. The two girls didn't talk for a few minutes.

Then Paris said, "I think Max might have another girlfriend."

"What? Why do you think that, Paris?" Bree asked. Bree looked very surprised. She sounded very surprised, too.

Paris said, "I might be wrong. But I think Max has another girlfriend where his grandparents live. That's why he goes to see them so much."

"I don't believe that. The two of you go steady," Bree said.

"So? Max knows he could date another girl there. I wouldn't find out about it," Paris said.

"I don't believe Max would do that. Max isn't that kind of guy. He wouldn't do that to you," Bree said.

"I think he would," Paris said.

"You're wrong. I'm sure of that," Bree said.

"But you can't really be sure of that. Can you?" Paris asked.

At first Bree didn't answer. But then she said, "No. I guess I can't be sure."

chapter 3

Later that night, Paris was in her bedroom. She was doing her homework. Paris's cell phone rang. It was Trish. She quickly answered it.

Trish said, "Hi, Paris." Trish was her cousin. Trish lived in Wayfield. Wayfield was about sixty miles from where Paris lived.

"Hi, Trish. It's great to hear from you. What have you been doing?" Paris said.

"Nothing much. Just the same old things. Too much homework. Too many tests. How about you?" Trish asked.

"About the same for me," Paris said.

"I can't talk long, Paris. So this is why I called. Saturday night Wayfield will play its homecoming game. And I want you to come," Trish said.

"I don't know if I can," Paris said. It sounded like fun. But Paris would have to find a way to get there.

"Why? Are you still dating that guy?" Trish asked.

"His name is Max. And I'm still dating him," Paris said.

"Do you have to go out with him every Saturday night?" Trish asked.

"No. I don't have to go out with him every Saturday night. He won't even be in town this weekend," Paris said.

"Good. Then you can come to visit me," Trish said.

"I don't know. I would need a way to

get there," Paris said.

"Your parents can bring you. They can spend the weekend here with my parents. My mom said she'll call your mom about it tomorrow. So will you come?" Trish asked.

"Sure. It sounds like fun," Paris said. Paris knew she might as well go. Max would be out of town. And she wouldn't have anything else to do.

Trish said, "It will be fun, Paris. Or at least it will be if we win. And I think we will. We have a great team. But there's one more thing."

"What?" Paris asked.

"I've found the perfect guy for you, Paris," Trish said.

"I go steady, Trish. You know that," Paris said.

"You know I don't think you should go steady," Trish said.

"You don't think anyone should go steady," Paris said.

Trish laughed. Then she said, "You're right about that. So what about it? Do you want to go out with this guy?"

"I go steady, Trish. That means I can't date someone else," Paris said.

"It means you shouldn't date someone else. It doesn't mean you can't date someone else," Trish said.

"You think that because you've never gone steady," Paris said.

"I know. But I'm too smart for that," Trish said. Then she laughed.

Paris said, "One day you'll find the perfect guy for you. And you'll want to go steady."

"Maybe. But that's a long time off," Trish said. Then she laughed again. This time Paris laughed, too.

Trish said, "Let me tell you about this

perfect guy I found for you. So listen."

"Okay," Paris said. She could listen. But that didn't mean she would date him.

Trish said, "His name is Blake. He's tall. He has blond hair. And he's very cute."

"I've seen some of the guys you think are cute, Trish. I didn't think all of them were cute," Paris said.

Trish laughed again. "Trust me on this, Paris. This guy is cute. I'm sure you'll like him," Trish said.

"You think he's so great. Why don't you date him?" Paris said.

"I said he's perfect for you, Paris. I didn't say he was perfect for me. So what do you say? Do you want me to set you up on a date with Blake? Or not?" Trish asked.

"I told you, Trish. But I'll tell you

again. I go steady with Max. You know I do," Paris said.

Trish said, "I know. I know. But what do you say? Do you want me to set the date up? Or not?"

"I don't think so," Paris said.

"You don't sound too sure about that, Paris," Trish said.

Paris didn't feel too sure about it, either.

Trish said, "Think about it, Paris. And think quickly. I need to tell Blake as soon as I can. So he won't make a date with someone else."

"Just forget about it, Trish. Why can't just the two of us go to the game? No guys," Paris said.

"That wouldn't be any fun, Paris. Think about dating Blake. I'll call you tomorrow night. You can tell me then what you want to do. But be sure it's *yes*," Trish said.

Then she hung up.

Paris knew she shouldn't even think about dating another guy. But she would think about it.

Maybe Trish was right after all. Maybe she should date Blake.

chapter
4

It was the next day. Paris sat in the lunchroom. She was waiting for Bree.

Bree hurried into the lunchroom. She got her lunch. And then she hurried over to the table. Bree sat down next to Paris.

"It's about time you got here," Paris said.

"I had to stay after class. I had a question about my homework," Bree said.

"Did you find out what you needed to know?" Paris asked.

"Yes. I have a lot of homework tonight," Bree said.

"Too bad," Paris said.

"What do you want to talk to me about? I'm sorry I didn't have a chance to talk this morning. But I had to get to class early," Bree said.

Paris had tried to talk to Bree before school started. "Why did you have to get to class early?" Paris asked.

"I had a question about that homework, too. So what do you want to talk to me about?" Bree asked again.

"My cousin Trish called last night. She wants me to visit her this weekend. She wants us to go to Wayfield's homecoming game," Paris said.

"That sounds like fun," Bree said.

"Trish said Wayfield has a great team this year," Paris said.

"I heard they did, too. Did you tell her

you would go to the game?" Bree asked.

"I told her I would. But—," Paris said.

"But what? You said Max would be out of town. So there isn't any reason why you can't go," Bree said.

"I haven't told you what else Trish said, Bree," Paris said.

"What?" Bree asked.

"Trish said she has found the perfect guy for me. His name is Blake. She wants me to go to the game with him," Paris said.

Bree looked surprised. "Why does Trish want you to go out with this perfect guy? Why doesn't she want to go out with him?" Bree asked.

"I asked Trish that," Paris said.

"What did she say?" Bree asked.

"She said he was perfect for me. But she didn't think he was perfect for her," Paris said.

"You aren't thinking about going out with him? Are you?" Bree asked.

"I told Trish that I go steady with Max," Paris said.

"Good. I am glad you told her that," Bree said.

"She already knew that. But she still wants me to go out with Blake," Paris said.

"You aren't thinking about going out with him? Are you?" Bree asked again.

"Maybe. Trish will call me tonight. I'll let her know then," Paris said.

Bree looked at Paris. And she didn't look happy.

"How can you even think about that? You go steady with Max," Bree said.

"I think Max is dating someone when he goes to see his grandparents. I think that's why he goes to see them so much," Paris said.

"You told me that yesterday, Paris. I didn't believe it then. And I don't believe it now. Max is too nice a guy to do that," Bree said.

Paris didn't say anything.

Bree said, "You can't date that guy, Paris. You shouldn't even think about doing it."

Paris still didn't say anything.

"Can't you go to the game with Trish? And not go with a guy?" Bree asked.

Paris said, "I don't know. Trish might already have a date. That might be why she wants me to have a date."

"Find out. But be sure you don't go with a date. You go steady with Max. Someone might see you and tell Max that you went out with another guy," Bree said.

"Would you tell him?" Paris asked.

Bree looked surprised. "No. I wouldn't

tell him. Why did you ask me that?" Bree asked.

"I didn't think you would tell him. I know that I wouldn't tell him. And I know that Trish wouldn't tell him. There's no one else who would know," Paris said.

So who would tell him?

chapter 5

Later that night, Paris's cell phone rang. Paris thought it was Trish. But it was Bree.

Paris said, "Why are you calling, Bree? I didn't think you could talk tonight."

"I don't have time to talk. But I wanted to talk to you again before Trish called," Bree said.

"Why?" Paris asked. But Paris knew why.

"Paris, you can't go out with that guy.

It wouldn't be fair to Max. So don't you dare tell Trish you'll date him," Bree said.

"I haven't made up my mind yet," Paris said.

"Then make up your mind to say *no*, Paris," Bree said.

Paris didn't say anything.

Bree said, "I have to hang up. Don't forget what I said, Paris. It wouldn't be fair to Max." Bree hung up.

Paris thought about what she should do. She didn't want to date another guy. But she believed that Max was dating someone else. So why shouldn't she date someone else, too?

Paris's cell phone rang. It was Trish.

Trish said, "My mom called your mom, Paris. So you have a way to come and see me. Do you want me to get you a date with Blake? You'd better say *yes*."

"I still don't know what to do," Paris said.

"Why? I told you Blake is cute. And he's perfect for you," Trish said.

"Yes. I know. You told me that. And I told you that I go steady with Max. That means we don't date other people," Paris said.

Trish laughed. Then she said, "Are you sure Max doesn't date other girls?"

Paris didn't answer.

"Well, Paris. Are you sure Max doesn't date other girls?" Trish asked.

"No. I'm not sure," Paris said.

She didn't want to tell Trish that. But she did. So she might as well tell Trish everything.

"I think Max is dating someone when he visits his grandparents. But I'm not sure," Paris said.

"How often does he go to see them?"

Trish asked.

"A lot. At least I think it's a lot. But Max says he doesn't go out with other girls," Paris said.

Trish laughed again. "And you believe him? I thought you were too smart for that, Paris. But maybe you aren't," Trish said.

That made Paris mad. "Someone might tell Max. That's why I don't want to date Blake."

Trish laughed again. She said, "The only people you know here are my parents and me. And we won't tell Max. Blake doesn't know Max. So Blake won't tell him. Who would tell him?"

"I don't know. I'm just worried that someone might," Paris said.

"No one will tell him unless you do. You won't tell Max. Will you?" Trish said.

"No," Paris said.

Trish said, "Then no one will tell Max. So there's no reason why you can't date Blake. I'll call him tonight."

Paris didn't say anything. She still wasn't sure what she should do.

Trish said, "Do what you want to do, Paris. Let Max date some girl at his grandparents. And you can just sit at home by yourself."

Paris didn't like what Trish said. But she did think Max was dating someone else. So why should she sit at home by herself?

Paris said, "Okay, Trish. Call Blake and set up the date for me."

"Great, Paris. You're doing the right thing. I'll call Blake as soon as I hang up. I'll see you this weekend," Trish said.

Paris wasn't sure she'd done the right thing. Max might find out.

But who would tell him?

chapter

6

The next morning, Paris had just gotten to school. Bree was waiting for her just outside.

"Did Trish call you last night?" Bree asked.

"Yes," Paris said.

Bree looked around. Then she looked at Paris. "I wanted to make sure no one could hear us. So what did you tell Trish? Did you tell her you didn't want to go out with that guy?"

Paris knew Bree wouldn't like what

she told Trish. So she didn't want to answer Bree.

Bree looked at her with a surprised look on her face. "You didn't? Please tell me you told Trish no," Bree said.

"I said *yes*," Paris said.

"Why? Do you really want to go out with him, Paris?" Bree asked.

"I don't know. I haven't met him yet. Trish thought he was perfect for me," Paris said.

"Is that why you said you would go out with him?" Bree asked.

"No. I told Trish that I think Max might be dating another girl. She thought he might be, too. And she said I shouldn't sit at home by myself," Paris said.

"How would Trish know what Max is doing? She doesn't even know him," Bree said.

Bree didn't look pleased with Paris. And she didn't sound pleased with Paris either.

"I don't care. I'll go out with Blake. And I'll have a good time," Paris said.

"You'll have a bad time after someone tells Max about it. And someone will. You can't keep something like that a secret," Bree said.

"I won't see anyone there who knows me or Max. So he'll never find out. Unless you tell him," Paris said.

"You aren't being fair to Max, Paris. Someone should tell him. But he won't find out from me," Bree turned around. Then she quickly went into the school.

Paris knew Bree was mad at her. She was sorry that Bree was mad. But she would still go out with Blake.

Paris's cell phone rang. It was Trish.

"Hi. I'm glad you called. But talk quickly. It's almost time for school to start," Paris said.

"Okay. This is why I called. I just saw Blake at school. He said that he would love to go out with you. So the date is all set," Trish said.

"Great," Paris said. But she wasn't really sure it was great. She couldn't back out of the date now.

Trish said, "I'm glad you still want to date Blake. See you this weekend. And have fun at school today."

Trish laughed. Then she hung up. Paris started to walk into the school. Max wouldn't find out about it. Would he?

chapter 7

It was Saturday night. Paris sat in the stands at the Wayfield game. She was with Blake. Trish was at the game, too. But Trish and her date weren't sitting with Paris and Blake.

Wayfield had just scored a touchdown. Paris and Blake stood up and cheered. Then they sat back down.

Blake said, "What a game."

"Yes. What a game," Paris said.

The game was great. But Paris wasn't having a great time. She liked Blake. He was nice. But she wanted to be with Max, not Blake.

Only a few minutes went by. Then Wayfield scored another touchdown. That made four.

Blake said, "I know we have a great team. But I can't believe we've scored so many touchdowns."

"I wish my team would score that many. Two is the most my team has scored in one game," Paris said.

"Too bad. I like it when a team scores a lot of touchdowns. And I'm glad my team did tonight," Blake said.

"I'm glad they did, too," Paris said.

She hoped the team would score again. But only a few minutes were left in the game.

It wasn't long until the game was over. Wayfield won 31–14.

Paris liked football games. But she

was glad this game was over. Paris and Blake started to walk to Blake's car.

Blake said, "This has been fun, Paris. I sure am glad Trish set up this date with you."

"Me, too," Paris said. But she wasn't glad.

Blake said, "You need to come back to visit Trish soon. So we can go to another game."

"That sounds like fun," Paris said. But she just said that to be nice.

"Do you come to visit Trish a lot?" Blake asked.

"No. Not a lot," Paris said.

"Maybe you can come and visit more now. So we can date," Blake said.

"Maybe so," Paris said. But she didn't think she would.

Blake was nice. But Paris didn't think Blake was perfect for her. She wanted to be with Max. What was Max doing? Did he have a date?

Blake said, "This is the biggest crowd at a game all year. I don't think some of them have been to our other games. But this is homecoming. So I guess that's why so many people are here."

"A lot of people go to homecoming at my school too," Paris said.

Paris felt as though someone was staring at her. Trish was the only person she knew. And Trish wouldn't have a reason to stare at her.

But that feeling didn't go away.

Paris had to know if someone really was staring at her. And if so, who? Paris stopped walking. Blake stopped walking, too.

Blake asked, "Is something wrong, Paris?"

"No. I just want to look for Trish," Paris said. But that wasn't true. Paris just wanted a chance to look around. She had to find out if someone was staring at her.

Paris turned around. She looked behind her. She couldn't believe who she saw. It was Max. He stared right at her. He was with an older man and woman. Paris thought they must be his grandparents.

So Max didn't have a date. But he now knew that Paris did.

Why had she come with another guy?

chapter 8

It was Monday morning. Paris waited outside the school. She looked for Max. She didn't see him. But she did see Bree. Bree stood near the front door.

Paris hurried over to Bree.

"Bree, have you seen Max?" she asked.

"What's wrong, Paris? You don't look well. Are you all right?" Bree asked.

Bree had a worried look on her face.

Paris said, "Max was at the game, too. I think he was there with his grandparents. And he saw me with Blake."

"Oh, no. Why didn't you call me?" Bree asked.

"I didn't want to use my phone. I tried to call Max. But he didn't answer. I left him a lot of messages. But he didn't call," Paris said.

"Max walked into school right before you got here," Bree said.

"Thanks, Bree. I can't talk now. I have to find Max," Paris said.

Paris hurried into the school. She walked quickly down the hall.

At first Paris didn't see Max. But then she saw him. He stood at his locker. She hurried over to talk with him.

"What do you want?" Max asked. He looked mad. And he sounded mad, too.

"I want to talk to you about Saturday night," Paris said.

"We don't have anything to talk about, Paris. Not now. Not ever," Max said.

"I wanted to talk to you at the game. But I couldn't," Paris said.

Max said, "No. You couldn't. I went to see my cousin play on the other team. I went to the game with my grandparents. But you went with a date."

Paris wished she hadn't gone with Blake.

Max said, "I thought we went steady. But you had a date with another guy."

"It was the first time I ever went out with him. My cousin Trish got me the date," Paris said.

"I don't care if it was the first time you went out with him. And I don't care who got you the date. I only care that you had a date with him," Max said.

Paris said, "I wouldn't have gone out with him. But I thought you were dating a girl where your grandparents live. And I thought that was why you went to see them so much."

Max's face got very red. And Paris knew he was very mad.

"I can't believe you. I go to see my grandparents because I care about *them*," Max said.

"I'm sorry, Max. I really am. But I really did think you were dating a girl there," Paris said.

Max said, "Why did you think that? I was going steady with you. I didn't want to date anyone but you. But not now. I don't want to date you ever again."

"Don't say that, Max. I promise I won't date another guy again," Paris said.

Max said, "It's too late, Paris. I trusted you. But now I know I can't trust you."

"You can trust me, Max. I promise you can. Give me another chance," Paris said.

"It's over, Paris. You wanted to date other guys. Well now you can," Max said.

Max slammed his locker shut. And he walked away from Paris.

Paris had been so sure that no one would tell Max. And she was right. No one had. But no one had to tell Max. He'd seen her himself.

Paris didn't think she could trust Max. But now Max knew he couldn't trust her.

Max was right about that.

consider this...

1. What would you do if you thought that your boyfriend/girlfriend was dating someone else?

2. How might Max have handled visiting his grandparents differently?

3. What is Paris most afraid of? How does Trish make it worse?

4. What might Blake have said if he turned around and saw Max at the game?

5. What would you do if you found out that your friend was cheating?